/50

MR. PEALE'S BONES

by Tracey West

SILVER MOON PRESS

MR. PEALE'S BONES

The publisher would like to thank Clare Flemming
of the American Museum of Natural History for her help
in preparing the Historical Postscript.

For information contact
Silver Moon Press,
126 Fifth Avenue, Suite 803
New York, New York 10011
(800) 874-3320

Design: John J.H. Kim
Cover: Nan Golub

Library of Congress Cataloging-in-Publication Data

West, Tracey, 1965-
Mr. Peale's Bones / by Tracey West. -- 1st ed.
p. cm. -- (Stories of the States)
Summary: An eleven-year-old boy living in New York State joins
the expedition of nineteenth-century artist and scientist, Charles
Willson Peale, to dig for mammoth bones on a nearby farm.
ISBN 1-881889-50-5 : $12.95
1. Peale, Charles Willson, 1741-1827--Juvenile fiction. [1. Peale,
Charles Willson, 1741-1827--Fiction. 2. Archaeology--Fiction. 3.
Fathers and sons--Fiction. 4. Mammoth--Fiction.]
I. Title. II. Series.
PZ7.W5197Mr 1994
[Fic]--dc20   93-41620

10 9 8 7 6 5 4 3 2 1

Printed in the USA

TABLE OF CONTENTS

CHAPTER ONE
August 4, 1801

"WILL FINCH! LET'S HAVE SOME MORE water here!"

Will hoisted the clay water jug higher. *Water, Will Finch! More water!* Those words had been spoken to him so many times in the last five weeks that they were all he heard in his sleep at night.

Will willed his legs to go faster. This was the third haying season he had spent working on his Uncle Martin's farm. Because he was the youngest member of the family and still too young to wield a scythe, he had been given the task of water boy. From the first rays of light until noon, he made endless trips from the well to his uncle and cousins as they worked in the field.

"Young Will's here at last! I'm afraid the sun has stolen the last drop of water in my body," Peter

Ketcham said. Peter set down his heavy scythe and took the jug. Will's oldest cousin was tall, with arms strong from years of farmwork. His linen shirt was drenched in sweat.

"Don't drink it all down, brother," Daniel Ketcham said.

He was fourteen, two years younger than his brother, but he looked as though he could handle any task that Peter could.

Daniel took a long drink. Watching him, Will ran his tongue across his own dry lips.

Daniel eyed him. "Will, you look as though you've been cutting the hay with the rest of us, and you've only been carrying water. You've barely the strength of a boy of eight."

"You know I'm eleven," Will said weakly. He was short for his age, with arms and legs as thin as kindling, his Uncle Martin always said.

"Leave the boy alone, Daniel," Peter said. "It will be two years before he's expected to keep up in the fields with us. I'm sure Will will grow to be a strong boy."

"No doubt he'll grow more like his father instead," Daniel replied.

Will felt his ears burn with shame. Peter started to speak, but the deep voice of Will's uncle interrupted. "Back to work, boys! It's almost noon!" Martin Ketcham called from across the field. "Will, bring me the grindstone. My scythe needs sharpening."

Daniel and Peter picked up their scythes. As they left, Daniel turned to Will and said in a low voice, "Be careful the grindstone doesn't crush you under its weight."

The loud caw of a crow caused Will to look up. The large black bird circled in the bright blue sky above. Will stood, watching the crow until it flew out of sight into the Catskill Mountains to the north.

"Will! The grindstone!"

His uncle's voice brought Will back to earth, and he broke into a run.

Despite the hard work of haying, the morning flew by. Soon enough, Will heard his cousins let out a yell as his Aunt Rebecca came to the field carrying the dinner basket. The sun was high in the sky. Noontime.

Uncle Martin kissed his wife on the cheek. "I hope you've brought enough food in this basket."

Aunt Rebecca smiled. "I'd be foolish not to." She spread a cloth on the ground and began to take food out of the basket — salted pork, hunks of bread and cheese, and a jug of apple cider.

"Meat and cheese again. A meal fit for a president," Peter joked.

"Only the best meal during haying," Aunt

Rebecca replied. "For you, too, Will. There's more work to be done this afternoon. You'll need your strength."

Will had already taken a large bite of bread and cheese. He stopped, remembering his manners. "Thank you for bringing dinner out, Aunt Rebecca."

"I've brought more than dinner, Will," Aunt Rebecca said, her eyes shining. "I've brought more news of the mammoth."

"The mammoth!" Will's eyes gleamed in the noonday sun.

Daniel laughed. "Ma, don't get Will too excited. He's already liable to faint from exhaustion. We need what strength he has left to help us with the raking."

"If I recall, you were the first one at the Hudson River days ago to watch the delivery of Mr. Peale's equipment, Daniel. Will's not the only one on this farm who's excited," Aunt Rebecca said.

Daniel flushed with embarrassment, and Will flashed his aunt a grateful smile. More news of the mammoth! This was a subject Will never tired of. It had made the weeks of haying a little easier.

Everyone in Newburgh had heard of the giant bones that John Masten had discovered on his farm in Ulster County. For weeks, Will had gathered bits and pieces of news about the bones after the Sunday church services. Some said that they were the bones of a mammoth creature that may have walked the earth before the Great Flood described in the Bible. Others said this idea was blasphemy, but most people agreed that the bones belonged to no living species.

When Masten put the bones on view in his barn, Will prayed they would be able to see them. Fortunately, everyone in Newburgh, including Will's uncle, had wanted to see the bones. Will remembered when Uncle Martin had taken him and his cousins to the Masten farms before spring planting. The pile of giant bones was dirty, and many were broken, but that didn't matter to Will. In his mind, he tried to reconstruct what such a creature might have looked like. The bones were like pieces of a puzzle waiting for someone to put them together.

And now it looked as though that someone was Charles Willson Peale. A few weeks ago, Will heard that the noted scientist had traveled all the way to Newburgh from Philadelphia to view the bones. He had arranged with Masten to dig up the land to find the mammoth's complete skeleton. Peale had even asked for help from the President of the United States, Thomas Jefferson.

Will could hardly wait for the digging to begin. The Ketchams thought Will was just excited about the thought of a giant beast, but it was more than that. Will knew he was destined to farm his uncle's land one day, but secretly he longed to be a scientist like Charles Willson Peale, or the great patriot Benjamin Franklin.

"Aunt Rebecca, what's the news of the mammoth today?" Will asked eagerly.

"Well, Mr. Masten says the bones are buried in a marl pit under twelve feet of water. But the army equipment President Jefferson sent isn't strong enough to pump the water out of the pit," Aunt Rebecca said.

Will's heart sank. "Does that mean the expedition will be cancelled?" he asked.

Aunt Rebecca shook her head. "No. Mr. Peale has a solution. He's asked Simon Campbell, the millwright, to help him construct a contraption that will bail the water out of the pit."

Uncle Martin frowned. "Peale's going to keep Campbell occupied during the busiest season of the year. We'd all be better off taking care of our farms than worrying about a bunch of old bones."

"But it's science, Uncle Martin," Will said, too excited to check his words. "It's important to study things like the mammoth bones."

"Learning doesn't put food on the table. Hard work does," Uncle Martin said gruffly. "Hard work is what's made this farm one of the most prosperous in the county. That's why we sell our wheat crop to England while most farmers can grow only enough for themselves."

Will lowered his eyes. It was stupid of him to anger his uncle. But all Uncle Martin thought of was this farm. He rarely looked beyond his own plot of land.

Daniel jumped on the chance to rile Will some more. "I've always said you need to do less thinking and more working, cousin." He sprang up and grabbed a small battered school primer from Will's trouser pocket. "Maybe this book is what's made you such a weakling, Will."

Will rose to his feet, his fists clenched. *He knows it's all I have in the world to call my own,* Will thought. *It's the only book to be found on this farm, and the only thing left of my mother.*

"I'll have that back, Daniel!" Will cried.

"What will you do, fight me for it?" Daniel was grinning.

"That's enough, both of you," Aunt Rebecca said. "Daniel, return the book to your cousin."

"Yes, Ma," Daniel said sheepishly.

Uncle Martin acted as if nothing had happened. "It's back to work for us, boys. Got to get this hay spread before dark."

Will took a last drink of cider. He held back as the others started toward the field. Aunt Rebecca put her arm around him. "Mr. Peale's work is important, Will. You're right to be interested in it."

Will watched his aunt walk back to the house. Mr. Peale's work *was* important. The haying would be finished soon, and then he could see the contraption Simon Campbell was making. He had to.

"Will, bring the water jug!" Peter called.

Will grabbed the jug and hurried toward the field.

CHAPTER TWO
August 5, 1801

T HE NEXT DAY PASSED WITHOUT FURTHER mention of the mammoth bones. Aunt Rebecca hadn't brought any more news about Mr. Peale with dinner, and Will, afraid to anger his uncle again, hadn't asked her.

At supper that night, Will picked up his fork as soon as grace was said and attacked his potatoes and cabbage. He was too young to wield a scythe but old enough to help his uncle and cousins spread the mown hay in the barn so it could be cured. The hard work increased Will's appetite tenfold.

"Looks like the haying will be done day-after-tomorrow," Uncle Martin announced at the supper table.

Daniel and Peter let out a cheer, and Will joined in, despite a stern look from Aunt Rebecca that told him such behavior wasn't for the supper table. The wheat still had to be harvested and threshed, the corn brought in, and the potatoes dug up, but the end of haying season meant the hardest work was done. Before long it would be winter, and Will could go back to the schoolroom.

They heard a knock on the door of the small pine house, and Will's aunt and uncle exchanged puzzled looks.

"Who could that be at such a late hour? It's nearly dark," Aunt Rebecca said. She went to open the door.

"Why, good evening, James."

Will dropped his fork on his plate as his father entered the doorway.

"Good evening, Rebecca. Good evening, Martin," James Finch said in his soft voice. He looked at Will. "Son."

"Good evening, sir," Will said, finding his voice.

Aunt Rebecca took the hat from Will's father's hands. "James, please have supper with us. There's plenty."

Uncle Martin shot an angry look at his wife that Will clearly saw, but James seemed not to notice.

"Thank you, I will." James pulled a chair from the corner and sat down at the table.

Everyone seated at the table stared at the food on their plates in silence. Will studied his father. James Finch was a slight man, a good two inches shorter even than sixteen-year-old Peter. His reddish hair framed a face that told the story of his life. On his chin was the jagged white scar delivered by a Redcoat's bayonet when James, still a youth, fought in George Washington's army. His left ear bore a more recent scar, one Will didn't like to think about. James got it trying to pull Will's mother, Betsy, from the fire that killed her.

The last time Will saw his father, there was frost on the ground. Will knew there must be an important reason for this visit. The room was too quiet. He wished someone would speak.

Uncle Martin cleared his throat. "I assume you've come to ask a favor of us, James. That's your usual reason for visiting."

"I've come for the boy," James said, leaning forward. "I've been hired to help with Mr. Peale's excavation. Simon Campbell needs a carpenter, and I want Will to come with me. I can't do the work without an assistant."

Daniel let out a low whistle, and even Will felt a small gasp escape him. His father's direct manner didn't surprise him; that was his way. But could his father really want him on the mammoth expedition? Will wasn't sure he had understood.

Uncle Martin stood up. "James, are you mad? We've got to get the haying in. We've fed and clothed the boy for three years, and we need his help now, as little as it is."

"Most farms in this county are only a day or two away from the end of haying season. I'm sure you are, too," James said. "I need Will. He knows his way with tools. From what I've seen, it will take a lot of hands to do what Mr. Peale wants."

Uncle Martin's cheeks grew red. "This doesn't surprise me, James. You expect us to take care of the boy for you, so you can fetch him when you need an extra pair of hands. Well, I won't have it."

"Martin, not here," Aunt Rebecca said.

James rose from his chair. "He's my boy."

"He certainly is," Uncle Martin said, his voice rising. "He's always either daydreaming or reading a book, never giving any effort to his real work."

Aunt Rebecca laid a hand on her husband's arm. "Martin, please. Think of Betsy," she said softly. "The haying's nearly in. Let him go."

Uncle Martin looked away. "Do as you want, James."

"Fine, then," James said. "I'll be back for Will in the morning."

Will excused himself from the table after

James left. *Why does he want me to go with him?* Will wondered. It didn't matter. Tomorrow, he was going to be part of a real scientific expedition.

The road to John Masten's farm was a rocky one, but enough people had traveled over it to keep the way fairly clear. Tall pine trees lined the path like soldiers at attention. Will bounced in the ramshackle wooden cart as James's horse pulled them along the path. The day was dry and hot, and Will was bursting with questions. Would they see the bones? Would they meet Mr. Peale? Will knew enough to keep to himself. Since his mother's death, Will's father had preferred silence to conversation.

"Farm's up ahead," James said without turning his head back.

Will strained to see. He remembered the farm from his trip to see the bones during the spring. His father was taking a route that led directly to Masten's fields.

Not long after, they came upon a crudely built shack and several tents set up about ten yards away. When they approached the shack, a finely dressed, white-haired man stepped out.

"You are Mr. Finch, our carpenter, I hope? We have great need of you," the man said. "I am Charles Willson Peale. And this must be your son.

You look so alike."

James nodded. "This is my boy, William."

"Splendid! I have always involved my sons in my work. They have proven to be invaluable. In fact, my son Rembrandt is assisting me on this expedition. I'll introduce you later." As he spoke, Peale grabbed their horse's reins and began to tie her to a nearby tree. Will had to run to keep up. Peale had to be in his sixties, but he had the energy of a man much younger.

Peale started toward the shack. "Come, both of you. Let us see the work that lies ahead of us."

Will followed his father into the shack. Another man about James's age was working wood on a lathe set up in the corner.

"Good day, Simon," James said. Will guessed this was Mr. Campbell, the millwright.

"Good day, James. I see you've brought Will with you."

"So he has," Peale said. "What do you think of our construction, Mr. Finch? I would value your opinion as a carpenter. Mr. Campbell and I built this just a few days ago."

"You built this shack? But you're a scientist," Will asked, too surprised to be polite.

"Yes, science is one of my specialties, and for science I will do whatever is necessary to accomplish the task at hand," Peale said. "And that includes building shacks." He walked to a wooden table and spread out some sheets of parchment. "Now let me show you what we must do."

Will peered over the table's edge. Mr. Peale had sketched a machine that featured a very large wheel at its center. It had to be the contraption Aunt Rebecca had spoken about, for clearing the water out of the pit.

Peale pointed to the sketches. "As you may already know, the bones we seek lie under twelve feet of water in a marl pit," he said. "We were able to procure a ship pump and several hand pumps from New York, but they are simply not powerful enough to do the job we need. So I designed this device." He pointed to a large wheel on his drawing that reminded Will of a water wheel. "As the wheel turns, these pulleys will also turn, lowering a string of buckets into the water. When the buckets come out of the pit, they will be filled with water."

"I see!" Will said, pressing in more closely to the drawings. "When the buckets reach the top of the pulley, they'll dump the water into that trough you've drawn. I suppose the trough will carry the water away to a safe place away from the marl pit."

"That's right, Will," Peale said, obviously pleased. "We've found a natural basin in which we can dump the water so that it won't drain back into the pit."

"That's ingenious," James said, a look of respect on his face. "I do have one question. This looks like a giant water wheel you've drawn. How can a water wheel turn on dry land?"

Peale smiled. "The wheel will be powered by the oldest source known on earth. Man!"

Will couldn't believe what he was hearing. "Do you mean that a person walking inside the wheel will make the wheel turn?"

"Precisely!"

"But where will you find enough men to power such a thing?" James asked.

"If my thinking is correct, we will have an abundance of curious parties willing to help us with our important work," Peale said. "If not, then I shall walk inside the wheel myself. Exercise is good for the body and the soul."

"It sounds like a task of *mammoth* proportions," James said. Will turned to look at his father. Had he actually told a joke? Will laughed.

"So it is!" Peale said. "And now, to work!"

CHAPTER 3
August 13, 1801

"YANKEE DOODLE WENT TO TOWN, A-RIDIN' on a pony ..."

Simon Campbell's pleasing tenor voice drifted through the makeshift camp, and Will couldn't help whistling along. Building the giant wheel was almost as hard as helping with the haying. But Simon's singing kept their spirits up as they tried again and again to get Mr. Peale's contraption working properly.

Rising twenty feet high on the left bank of the marl pit, the wheel was awesome. Scaffolding cut from wooden poles supported the contraption. Peale had designed the scaffolding in a cone shape, like a teepee. Four poles anchored the scaffolding: two on the one side of the bank and two on the other. A ladder led up to the point where the poles met, and from there hung the large pulley system that would lower the buckets into the pit.

After days of helping his father turn out bucket after bucket on the lathe, Will learned that Peale had orchestrated a trial run. Simon Campbell and Will's father had attached twenty buckets to the pulley at Peale's command, but the top of the pulley was too high. By the time the buckets dumped their loads, water had already seeped back into the marl pit.

Peale wasn't discouraged. He made some adjustments, only to have the buckets become entangled. Then Peale ordered that some of the buckets be removed. Will hoped the problem was solved. After all their labor, the wheel just *had* to work.

"Say there, Will, I think we're ready to give the wheel another try. What do you say?"

Will looked up into the kind face of Rembrandt Peale, Charles Willson Peale's second-eldest son. Rembrandt looked very much like his father, except his hair was sandy brown and his demeanor was quieter and more thoughtful. Will had liked Rembrandt from the moment he saw him.

"I hope this attempt is successful," Will said. "Tell me what I can do."

"I think it's time you took your turn inside the wheel," Rembrandt said.

Will was shocked. "Me? But I'm too small. I'd never be able to move such a big thing."

Rembrandt smiled. "Will, from what I have seen of you these past days, you can do anything you set your mind to. Besides, the principles behind the wheel's design are such that even a boy can turn it properly."

Will blushed. On his uncle's farm, no one noticed his hard work.

Just then, Peale walked up. The strain and hectic pace of the last few days seemed to have left no trace on him.

"Ah, Rembrandt, I see you are enlisting Will's help in turning the wheel," Peale said. "Let's not waste any time."

"Why are we always in such a hurry, Rembrandt?" Will asked as they walked around the pit to the wheel. "The bones have been here for thousands of years. Can't they wait a few days more for us to uncover them?"

"It's not that simple," Rembrandt said. "First, there is the expense. Once we get the wheel working, father will have to hire at least twenty-five men to dig in the pit and man the pulleys."

"But this is such an important expedition. Can't President Jefferson help?"

"I'm afraid not. The president has given us all the help he can already. The United States of

America is a new republic. There isn't much extra money right now, even for an important cause."

"Is money the only reason?" Will asked.

"Not by any means," Rembrandt said. "The other reason is the marl pit itself. When John Masten and his hands first began to dig for the bones, they weren't careful. The banks of the pit get softer every day, and no matter how fast we pump the water out, more will seep in. It's only a matter of days before the pit collapses and the bones are lost forever."

"I see," said Will. Turning the wheel took on a new importance now.

"Is everyone at the ready?" Peale called out.

"Ready!" Simon Campbell called from the base of the scaffolding.

"Ready!" James called. Will looked up. His father had climbed the ladder so he could monitor the buckets as they dumped water in the trough.

"Ready!" Rembrandt called when he arrived at his father's side.

Will took a deep breath and climbed into the wheel. "Ready, sir!"

"Let's begin!" Peale shouted from across the pit. "Will, keep the wheel running for five minutes. I need to measure the amount of water removed from the pit during a five-minute period."

Will steadied himself inside the wheel, then

began to walk the way he had seen his father and Simon do. With a creak, the wheel began to turn. Will couldn't see, but he could hear the pulleys turning and water splashing in the trough above.

What an odd sensation, Will thought. It was as though he were climbing a mountain with no hope of reaching the top. Rembrandt was right, though. The wheel moved fairly easily.

Left, right, left, right. Five minutes seemed to take forever. The task wasn't difficult, but Will wanted to know if the wheel was working.

Finally, he heard Peale's voice, closer this time. "That's enough for now, Will. We've done it!"

Will jumped off the still-turning wheel. Peale and Rembrandt had walked to the left bank. "You mean the wheel works, then?"

"Perfectly, my boy!"

"Hurrah!" Will shouted.

James Finch climbed down from the ladder. "It's as smooth as can be up there, sir." He was smiling.

"This is excellent," Peale said. He turned to Simon Campbell, who had just joined them. "Campbell, I will need twenty-five men as soon as possible. I suppose it is too late now for us to begin. First light tomorrow, then. I'll pay nine shillings a day."

Campbell nodded. "That's a fair price, sir. I'll

have no trouble finding the men."

Peale turned to James. "Of course, you and your boy are welcome to stay on."

Will looked at his father hopefully. James extended his hand to Peale. "We'd be honored to, sir."

Peale grinned. "Splendid! Let's see about supper, then."

Peale had arranged with Mrs. Masten to provide dinner and supper for their camp each day, and that night they dined well on roasted squirrel washed down with ale. Simon and James set out before dark to hire men for the next day's work.

On most days, Will and the men kept working until it was too dark to work anymore. At night, Rembrandt would usually sit up with a book in the candlelight, and Peale often stayed up late in the shack, poring over plans and refining them. Will usually fell asleep not long after his last bite of supper.

But tonight he was restless. It was twilight, and Peale had lighted a lantern and spread a large piece of parchment over a crude worktable he had built. Curious, Will cautiously approached the table.

"It's like a giant puzzle, Will," Peale said, without looking up from the paper.

That's just what I always said, Will thought to himself. *But no one understood me.* Will studied the paper. He knew Peale had sketched the bones he had purchased from Masten in June. Peale had taken the bones back to Philadelphia to study them.

"What kind of creature is the mammoth?" Will asked. Days ago he learned that Peale seemed happy to answer his questions. Will realized that he had spoken to Peale more than to his own father since the dig had begun.

"It is difficult to say," Peale replied. "There have been reports of these mammoth bones in other parts of America, but people cannot agree on the kind of animal they come from. They seem to belong to a creature like the elephants of India and Africa. In fact, some believe the mammoth still crashes through the American wilderness."

Will's eyes widened. "Do *you* believe that?"

Peale shook his head. "I cannot believe that such a large creature could go undetected, even in a country as vast as this. At any rate, the answers to many of these questions lie beneath the waters of the marl pit."

Will looked over at the pit. The murky waters seemed dark and mysterious under the moonlight and the flickering lantern. *What would they find there?* Will wondered. Tomorrow couldn't come soon enough to suit him.

CHAPTER FOUR
August 14, 1801

"THIS WATER IS COLDER THAN THE DEVIL!" Will couldn't help laughing. Simon and James had no trouble bringing workmen to the pit with a promise of nine shillings a day. But one by one, the men splashed into the waters of the marl pit, only to emerge wet and sputtering. They had gathered around Simon now.

"Even nine shillings isn't worth freezing for, Simon," one man complained.

Peale arrived on the scene. "What's this? Is a little cold too much for the strong men of New York State? I wouldn't have guessed it."

"Even the strongest man couldn't withstand that hellish pit," another man shouted.

"I see. And I suppose a limitless supply of grog wouldn't help to chase away the cold?" Peale asked.

At the mention of the spiced rum drink, the men quieted down. "That certainly would help."

"Splendid! The grog shall flow freely," Peale said. "Until then, I suggest we get on with our work."

Simon and James had been at the wheel since sunrise, and their efforts had an effect. The water was only knee-deep in some places. When James grew tired, Will took a turn relieving his father. They had to keep the wheel moving constantly, or the pit would just fill up again.

Will's heart pounded with excitement as the men picked up the shovels that had been donated by the army and once again entered the pit. The farmers were a "scruffy lot," as his aunt would say, but their muscles strained under their worn linen shirts, and Will could tell they were hard workers. Most of the men rolled up their trousers before they entered the sticky marl, and some wore wide-brimmed hats to keep out the sun.

At one point Will thought his legs might give out, but by afternoon, he lost all worry. Peale's first guess, that spectators would turn out to see the wheel, was right. Word about the project had spread quickly. It was harvesting time, but Will thought all of Ulster County must have turned out to watch the spectacle.

Men and boys lined up for a chance to work

the wheel. From the looks of the crowd, Will thought it would be days before he walked inside the wheel again.

Not that Will had time to be idle. He was helping James erect tents as shelter for the workmen when a cry rang out from the pit.

"Bones! We've found bones!"

Will and his father looked at one another, then dropped the tent poles they were holding and ran to the site.

Peale was leaning over the pit, looking down at two workmen. They had uncovered a mess of attached bones that seemed to be about two feet long. The bones were partially buried in the black mud that oozed from the side of the pit.

"These are the bones of the foot!" Peale said. "Don't pull them out of the mud yet. We'll have to dig around them so we can get them out while they're still attached."

As Peale spoke, however, Will could see that the black mud was quickly pushing down on the foot bones, which were in danger of sinking into the white shell marl at the bottom of the pit. Unless the men worked quickly, the bones might be lost forever.

Peale seemed to have noticed this, too. His face bore a look of frustration. "We must take them out now! Quickly!"

A crowd of workmen gathered. Two men dug at the mud with their shovels, while others carefully pulled the bones out one by one and handed them up to Peale.

"Are they broken?" Will asked, pushing his way to Peale's side.

"No, but they have separated from one another. They will be more difficult, though probably not impossible, to reconstruct."

Without thinking, Will reached out and touched a muddy bone. The bone was as thick as his arm, yet Peale had said it was part of the mammoth's foot.

"Excellent work, men! We must keep up the search!" Peale called out.

During the next few days, Will sometimes thought it was Peale's enthusiasm alone that kept the crew going. Digging in the pit wasn't easy work. Each day, the workmen struggled to stand upright on the oozy bottom of the pit. As the men dug, the banks of the pit continued to soften. Simon and James had to keep a careful eye on the supports of the scaffolding.

The pit gave up a few more treasures to the crew: some more small bones, some teeth, and a piece of something Peale said was the mammoth's tusk.

Peale rarely left the pit's edge, and if he did, it was to study sketches he had made in

Philadelphia.

"If we could only find the creature's jaw-bone," Peale would say, shaking his head. "Then we could complete the skeleton."

Even the farmers, who had been excited by the first sight of bones, were disappointed with the small pieces that were turning up. The missing jaw-bone was a prize that everyone hoped to find.

The August days were dry and hot, and Will found himself scrutinizing every corner of the pit, wishing there were some way he could make the muddy earth dry and stable. The banks would not be able to hold the scaffolding much longer. What would happen then? James would go back to his carpentry, and Will would be back at the farm, just like before. He couldn't bear the thought.

The afternoon air was thick and smelled like rain. There was a smaller crowd lined up to walk the wheel today, so Will decided to take a turn. After all, Peale had said that exercise was good for the soul.

Will was walking inside the wheel, pushing against the wood in front of him for support, when he heard a familiar voice.

"Is that little Will making the wheel turn all by himself?"

Will looked to the side to see the jeering face of his cousin Daniel. He had almost forgotten that look. With it, Will was was transported back to the farm, and his heart sank. *Just don't think about it,* Will told himself. He began to push faster.

"Will, I can't believe my eyes! This machine is amazing," Daniel said, sounding for once like he wasn't making fun of Will. "How does it work?"

Will eyed his cousin. Daniel looked genuinely interested. "You can do it," Will said. "Jump in as soon as I jump off. The wheel needs to keep moving."

Daniel did as Will said. "How did you get here?" Will asked.

"I came with Father," Daniel said. "It wasn't easy convincing him to come, but I did. I've heard the wheel won't be up much longer."

Will frowned. Just then, the sound of thunder growled ominously behind them. The afternoon sky was beginning to darken quickly.

"It can't rain!" Will cried. "The pit will fill up deeper than before. Mr. Peale will never find the jawbone." He couldn't expect Daniel to understand how he would feel if that happened.

Peale came running toward the wheel. "This may be it, Will. Keep the wheel moving. We've got to keep working," he called. Behind him, a white streak of lightning flashed over the Shawangunks Mountains.

Daniel was still inside the wheel, but he was looking at Will with wide eyes. "Was that Mr.

Peale? But he spoke to you —"

"I know, Daniel. You heard him. We've got to keep the wheel moving," Will called over a thunder clap.

Will looked into the pit. His father and Simon were in there now, digging with the other workmen. Peale was running around the pit's edge like a whirlwind, stirring the men into action.

Another sliver of lightning flashed in the distance. Will looked at the mountains, where black clouds were gathering quickly. They hadn't had a storm in weeks, and Will was sure they were finally due for one.

Will wasn't sure how much time passed as the crew raced the storm's approach. He and Daniel worked with other spectators to keep the wheel turning, as Peale had directed. Exhausted and covered with sweat, Will finally heard Rembrandt give a yell from his position at the drainage ditch.

"The storm's passing!"

Could it be true? The storm clouds seemed to be moving away from the mountains. Where the sky had been black, it was now a faint blue-gray.

"We beat the storm! It didn't rain!" Daniel was shouting. "It's a miracle."

Will flopped down on the dry ground. He wanted to share Daniel's excitement, but he couldn't. They may have beaten the storm, but they still hadn't found the jawbone. Masten's pit could not offer them that prize.

CHAPTER FIVE
August 17, 1801

THE NEXT DAY, WILL'S FEARS CAME TRUE. THE workmen had returned to work on the pit, but Peale gave them their pay and sent them on their way. Will saw Peale talking earnestly with Simon and James and ran toward them.

"And so I'm afraid we'll have to dismantle the wheel today," Peale was saying. "The banks of the pit just won't support it any longer."

"But what about the mammoth, Mr. Peale? We haven't found a complete skeleton yet," Will said.

"Will!" James scolded, but Peale held up his hand.

"A perfectly reasonable question, Mr. Finch. I appreciate the boy's enthusiasm," Peale said. "I have received word from my good friend Dr.

Galatian that a certain Captain Barber of Montgomery has found bones on his farmland, as well. The terrain is flat and not terribly wet. Our money and time will be better spent there."

Peale turned to James. "Of course, I should like your services again, Mr. Finch. And please bring young Will along. He has proven to be quite an asset to our expedition."

"Will we go to Montgomery today?" Will asked.

"Unfortunately, I will need some time to view the sight myself and find the best spot for our excavation," Peale said. "I hope to send for you in three or four days' time."

Will looked at his father. Would James accept the offer?

"We'll be honored to assist you again, Mr. Peale," James said.

Will breathed a sigh of relief. Their quest for the mammoth was not over yet.

It was late in the day when the site of the Masten excavation was finally cleared. James hooked his horse up to the small cart again. Weeks had passed since they had first traveled to Masten's farm, but to Will it seemed just like yesterday.

James was whistling as he urged the horse back down the rocky path. *His spirits seemed much brighter than on their trip to the farm*, Will thought. Still, his father was quiet, more like the father Will was used to. Even so, Will decided to risk asking a question.

"Father, are we going back to Uncle Martin's farm?" Will asked. They hadn't spoken about how the days waiting for Mr. Peale would be spent.

"Yes, Will. No doubt the wheat crop is ready for harvest. We owe it to your uncle to help him."

"Does that mean you'll be staying at the farm?" Will asked in surprise.

"Until Mr. Peale needs us," James said.

Will sat back in the cart and pondered this. Having his father nearby would help make up for Daniel's teasing.

Will gathered his courage. Somehow it was easier talking to the back of his father's head.

"Father, what will happen when the excavation is finally over?"

"I will continue my carpentry, and you will return to the farm," James said simply.

These were the words Will had been dreading. His knuckles were white as he gripped the edge of the cart. Will leaned forward. "But father, I've been thinking. I could be your apprentice. I'm old enough. I could stay with you at the shop. Uncle Martin doesn't need me at the farm. I'm too small. And you said yourself that I'm good with my hands."

James's shoulders sank. He slowed the horse to a stop and turned to face Will. "Son, I would like nothing better to have you as an apprentice. I'm proud of the way you've worked with Mr. Peale these two weeks. But a boy needs a family, not a man whose only other companion is the ghost of his past."

Will looked at his father's worn face. "You are my family."

"I am not enough." James urged the horse ahead.

They finished their journey in silence. Knowing his father wanted him was a comfort that sealed an ache Will had long held in his heart. But it wasn't comfort enough. When the mammoth skeleton was complete, his father would be gone again.

From the moment they arrived at the Ketcham farm, however, Will had little time for worry. Daniel had told the family about Will's work at the great wheel, and Aunt Rebecca and Peter wanted to hear all the details of the adventure so far. Even Uncle Martin viewed Will and his father with cautious respect.

The next morning, there was no time for talk. There were wheat fields to be harvested and threshed. The days that followed seemed to fly as

Will spent hours using the old wooden flail to separate the wheat's grain from the stalk. Usually, Will hated threshing as much as haying, but this year he was grateful. It kept his mind occupied while they waited for news from Mr. Peale.

James spent the days in the fields helping Uncle Martin with the harvesting. Will saw him mostly at suppertime, where he ate without speaking to anyone at the table.

Then one morning, James came into the barn, his face set in a wide grin. "Best put down that flail, son. Simon Campbell's just been 'round. Mr. Peale needs our help."

CHAPTER 6
August 27, 1801

"**H**OW'S THAT DRAINAGE DITCH COMING along, Will?"

Will wiped the sweat from his brow and looked up at Mr. Peale. "Just fine, sir."

"Splendid!" Peale cried. "There are mammoth bones in this soil, and I'm anxious to find them. There are many people counting on me to produce a complete mammoth skeleton — and our president is one of them. We've spent a lot of time and money so far, and failure would be a blow to the future of scientific expeditions in this country."

Will's eyes grew wide. All along, he had been worrying about returning to the farm. But listening to Mr. Peale, he realized that the expedition was important not just to Will, but to the world. The thought was a little frightening.

"Take a short rest, Will," Peale said, interrupting Will's thoughts. "I'd like to show you my latest invention."

Will climbed from the ditch and followed Mr. Peale toward a small group of workmen, who were each holding long metal poles with pointed tips. Peale asked one of the men to hand him a pole.

"Captain Barber couldn't pinpoint exactly where the best bones might be buried," Peale explained. "We would waste time and effort digging over all of Barber's land. That's where my poles come in."

"What can they do?" Will asked.

Peale handed a pole to Will. "Thrust the pole into the ground here. The earth is soft."

Will did as instructed. He was able to sink the pole about halfway into the ground.

"Did you strike anything?" Peale asked.

"I don't think so," Will said.

"Try again!"

Will picked another spot. This time, he felt something. "I've struck something soft — like rotten wood."

"Excellent!" Peale said. "You've got the hang of it. With careful judgment, it's also possible to tell if you've struck hard stone, or the slightly softer texture of mammoth bone. I've been instructing the crew, and they seem to have picked up the technique."

"I see," Will said. "So when you hit bone beneath the ground, you'll know that you're digging in the right place."

"Exactly!" Peale said. "That's why you're digging a drainage ditch. We located some bones this morning, and we need to drain the surface water from the area before we can start excavating. In fact, you should get back to the ditch now. There's no time to waste."

Will returned to the ditch feeling a little better about the back-breaking work he was doing. When he drove his shovel into the ground, he dug up another large chunk of dirt. Will decided that scientific study sometimes felt just like farmwork.

Peale's way of constantly coming up with ingenious solutions to the problems of the expedition fascinated Will. If there were a way to do something better or faster, Peale would think of it. *Even if I could study and become a scientist, I doubt I could ever be as smart as Mr. Peale*, Will thought.

James saw Will working in the ditch and smiled. "Keep digging, son. I dare say we'll have plenty of earth to move in the days ahead."

Will's father was right about that. For three days, Will helped as they began a careful excavation of the area. Early on, a promising find had been made when one of the men dug up a well-preserved toe bone.

Peale seemed excited. "My hope is to find a complete skeleton in its original position, with the bones undisturbed. Perhaps this is where we shall find it."

With each sign of success, Will dug a little harder and a little faster. He could almost picture the hulking skeleton underneath the dirt.

But no skeleton was found, though the search produced two mammoth tusks that were identifiable but rotten. Will marvelled at their size. Other bones were found, too, but they were scattered about and were often badly decayed.

If Peale was disappointed, he didn't show it. He moved the crew to a different site on Captain Barber's farm, on a parcel of land farmed by a man named Peter Millspaw. Millspaw, too, had reported finding fragments of bone and coarse hair on the ground's surface.

On September first, they began to search the new sight. Peale had marked an area for excavation thirty-six by forty-five feet in size; it was a marshy, rotting-timber forest where the ground was covered with spreading roots. By this time, Will was digging as long and hard as the grown men in the crew.

"Will, this is hard work for a boy," James told him on their first night at the new site. Will had collapsed, exhausted, inside their tent. "You can go back to the farm anytime you want."

Will sat up. "Please, Father, I want to keep on until the work is finished." *And I want to stay on with you as long as I can*, Will thought, though he couldn't say it aloud.

James ran his hand along his sunburnt chin. "You remind me of your mother, Will. She wouldn't stop until she got the job done right." He stood up and began pacing. "Will, I've done a lot of thinking. I've spoken to your uncle about it, and if you want to spend the winter with me at my shop, well, we both agreed it might be a good idea."

Will rose and threw his arms around his father. "Thank you. I'll be a good apprentice."

James shook his head. "I'll use your help, but not as my apprentice. You'll still spend spring on the farm with your uncle, but I think you should go back to the schoolroom this winter. It's what your mother would have wanted. Besides, as Mr. Peale would say, the mind needs as much exercise as the body."

"How right you are, Mr. Finch." Peale stepped out of the darkness. Sometimes Will thought the leaders of the expedition went without sleep altogether. "I think our bodies have seen a great deal of exercise these past weeks, enough to last Will here through the winter."

"Will we ever find enough bones to complete a whole skeleton, Mr. Peale? Will we find a complete jawbone?" Will asked.

Peale's eyes shone in the darkness. "I certainly hope we do, Will. But I think we shall succeed. We've come too far not to."

"It's late, son," James said as Peale walked away. "We've got much to do in the morning."

"I'm glad about this winter, father," Will said sleepily.

"I am, too, Will," James said. "But before the cold sets in, we've got a giant to find!"

CHAPTER SEVEN
"We Have One Last Chance."

"WE CAN'T CONTINUE THE DIG MUCH longer," Peale told the crew one night. "I've barely got money left for another week's pay for all of you."

"I'll dig for free! We're too close to stop now!" one of the men cried.

This remark caused an uproar of laughter from the workers. "Don't speak for all of us, Wilkins," a blond farmer cheerfully called out.

"That's a generous offer," Peale said, "but I'm afraid it doesn't matter. There are too many expenses involved, and I'm due back in Philadelphia soon anyway."

Will didn't want to believe what he was hearing, but it was no surprise. A few days ago, they had moved to another site, but all they had unearthed was a piece of a mammoth's vertebra, a small part of the creature's spine. Will had nearly cried with disappointment.

"We have one last chance," Peale said. "We've located another site on Millspaw's land. We'll move the expedition there in the morning."

The thought of their last chance kept Will's sore arms moving during the following days of what seemed like endless hours of digging. Summer was coming to a close, and the nights were growing colder. He was beginning to miss his straw mattress at the farmhouse, bedbugs and all.

The rest of the crew was just as uncomfortable, but for some reason, Will noticed their spirits were high. It may have been Mr. Peale's undying enthusiasm, but Will felt it was more than that. It was as though they had all traveled far together on a long journey and were at last almost in sight of their destination. They couldn't give in to disappointment now. Will gritted his teeth and lifted another shovelful of dirt. If the farmers could keep their spirits up, so could he.

September eleventh dawned a bright, clear day. After a morning meal of pan biscuits and milk, Will stretched and picked up his shovel. *At least the days aren't so hot*, Will thought. *It makes the hard work more bearable.*

Will lowered himself down into a soggy pit

the men had begun the day before. It was only about three feet deep. When he stabbed his shovel into the loose ground, he began whistling "Yankee Doodle," the way he had at the marl pit when they were first building the wheel. James and the other men joined in.

Sometime before noon, a shout from Rembrandt disturbed Will's rhythmic digging. Will craned his neck and looked out of the pit. Rembrandt was standing about eighty feet away. He was waving his pointed rod in the air excitedly.

"Father, I think I've found something! Something big!"

Peale ran toward his son, and Will scrambled up out of the pit after him. He arrived, out of breath, as Rembrandt was talking to his father.

"From what I can tell, there are some very large bones under here, larger than we've uncovered before. And there is an *abundance* of them," Rembrandt was saying excitedly.

Peale was making a careful study of the area. It was covered with scrubby trees and bushes.

"There's much to be done," Peale said. He called back to the crew. "Men, abandon that site! I think we've found what we've been looking for."

For the next few hours, the men worked faster than Will had ever seen. Will helped yank stubborn roots and bushes from the ground as the men cleared away the trees. The top layer of sod was entwined with roots that the crew furiously tore away.

Beneath the roots and sod was soft, loamy soil. *And bones,* Will wished silently, *please let there be bones.*

"Dig carefully," Peale warned. "The bones are not far down."

Will stood by James's side and began to dig. Dirt flew around them and settled over the work area like a brown cloud. James's eyes were bright, and his forehead glistened with sweat. Will supposed he looked the same way, but he hardly felt the work now. The shovel seemed light as air.

The first triumphant shout startled Will more than he thought it would. It came from his father.

"There's something over here, Mr. Peale. And it's big!"

Will looked at the giant bone his father uncovered, and he gasped in awe. It was almost pure white, and as more dirt fell away, Will saw that it was almost as long as he was tall.

"It's a shoulder bone!" Peale said excitedly. "And a beautiful one, at that. Perhaps our jawbone is not too far off."

The digging now didn't even seem like work. Not long after, two leg bones were discovered, larger even than the shoulder bone. And finally, Peale got his long sought-after prize.

He was examining a curved white bone one of the men had just uncovered. "At long last," Peale said breathlessly, "a complete lower jaw! Gracious God, what a jaw! How many animals have been crushed between it!" Peale was visibly more excited than he had been at any point during the expedition.

"Hurrah!" A cry erupted from the crew so loud that Will imagined it could be heard all the way back to England. The workmen were slapping each other on the back and laughing.

"We did it, father! We did it!" Will yelled.

"That's right, Will!" James shouted above the din. He lifted Will into the air. "We did it — all of us!"

By the next day, it was evident that the site had produced almost a complete mammoth skeleton. The camp was quiet now. The expedition had been a success, and Mr. Peale was taking the bones back to Philadelphia.

Peale had spread the bones out on a dry patch of grass. Looking at the different pieces, it wasn't difficult for Will to see how the mammoth might have looked. Closing his eyes, he reached out and touched the smooth shoulder bone his father had uncovered. In his mind, he saw the shaggy brown beast Mr. Peale had described, crashing through the Shawangunk Mountains as small animals scattered out of its path. *What would it have been like to have lived so long ago?* Will wondered. Touching the bones almost made him feel as if he had been there.

"It's a wonderful feeling, isn't it Will?"

Will opened his eyes and turned to face Mr. Peale. "What will happen to the bones now?"

"I'll take them back to my museum in Philadelphia. The skeleton John Masten found is almost as complete as this one. Between the two, we should be able to recreate the giant beast. Rembrandt can carve from wood whatever bones we are missing."

"They are wonderful bones," Will said, stroking the shoulder blade for the last time.

"They certainly are. And I thank you for your help in finding them, Will," Peale said. "Just think, the whole world will soon know of our discovery here."

Will smiled. Even if he never heard news of the mammoth again, he would never forget the summer he spent digging for a giant's bones with Charles Willson Peale.

CHAPTER EIGHT
The Largest of Terrestrial Beings!

WILL DUCKED AS A SNOWBALL WHIZZED BY his ear.

"Daniel," Will muttered. Ignoring his frozen hands, he quickly formed a snowball of his own and let it sail toward his cousin.

"Missed me, Will Finch!" Daniel said, laughing.

Will sighed. He missed life on the Ketcham farm, but seeing Daniel in the schoolroom every day made him glad he didn't have to go back until late spring.

"Not today, Daniel. I've got important news for Father."

Daniel's jeer turned to a look of respect. "I forgot. Give my best to Uncle James."

Will's feet crunched on the trail as he walked

the half mile to his father's small cabin. He buried his hands in his pockets for warmth. Beneath his wool coat, he felt the soft package he had tucked there. The road home seemed twice as long today. Will could hardly wait to share his news.

Finally, the wood cabin was in view. Will opened the door and welcomed the warmth from the fireplace. Throwing his coat aside, he ran to his father's worktable.

"Father, wait until you see what I've brought home," Will said. He presented the small package to his father. It was a carefully folded letter.

"Mistress Belnap received a letter from her cousin in Philadelphia. She's seen the mammoth — all of it," Will said.

"What do you mean?" James raised an eyebrow.

Will took the letter from his father. "Mistress Belnap's cousin says that Mr. Peale put a grand announcement in the newspaper. He and Rembrandt finished the skeleton, and they put it on public view. Mr. Peale billed it as 'The Largest of Terrestrial Beings.' That means beings that walked the earth. I asked Mistress Belnap."

"I see," James said. "How impressive."

"There's more," Will said. "She says that Peale plans to take the mammoth on a tour of the world. She says the mammoth is one of the most important scientific finds of the century." Will sighed. "She makes it sound so important."

"It is important, and you must never forget that you played some part in it," James said. His voice grew softer. "Will, after your mother died, I admit I didn't know you too well. But the boy I spent the summer with was determined and intelligent. I think you can accomplish anything you put your mind to, son."

Hearing those words was for Will more important than helping to uncover an ancient gigantic beast. He smiled. "Father, I'm glad to be spending the winter with you. But I'll be glad to get back to the farm."

James looked puzzled. "I thought you hated farm work, Will."

"I do," Will said, a twinkle in his eye. "But who knows what we might find among Aunt Rebecca's cabbages. Maybe we'll find a mammoth of our own!"

Will Finch and his family are fictional characters. But Charles Willson Peale was a real person, and his expedition is an important part of United States history.

Peale began his expedition in the summer of 1801. He did purchase the first bones from John Masten, and he did hire a wheelwright named Simon Campbell to help him build the giant wheel used to drain the pit.

In Peale's diary, he writes of hiring a carpenter to help build the wheel, and twenty-five men to work in the pit. Because most farmers in the early nineteenth century would have been too busy to leave their fields to work on Peale's dig, the author invented James Finch, a skilled carpenter who was a loner without a family to support.

Years after the dig, Charles Willson Peale painted a scene of the expedition, showing the crew working against the approaching storm. In the painting, many boys about Will's age can be seen working on the dig. It's only a guess, but it's likely that many of them were just as curious about the contraption and the man behind it, Charles Willson Peale.

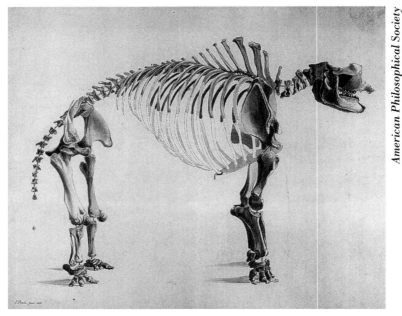

*Once Peale's mastodon skeleton was recovered from upstate
New York, it was assembled at a museum in Philadelphia.
Artists were then able to make drawings of the "great
beast" for other scientists.*

Peale's Mammoth

After leaving Orange County, Peale took the
bones back to his museum in Philadelphia. He
kept the bones from the Masten site and the
Millspaw site separate and began to piece the
skeletons together. Peale had nothing to guide
him. The only other fossil skeleton ever found
and reassembled was in Spain.

Eventually, Peale was able to make two
skeletons from the piles of bones. As he built the
first skeleton, excitement grew around the country. Everyone began to use the word "mammoth."

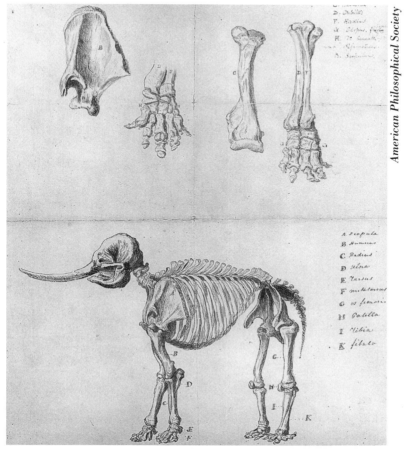

Often, the drawings made of the reassembled mastodon skeleton showed specific parts of the Ice-Age mammal's anatomy — bones of the foot and leg, for example.

One baker sold "Mammoth Bread," and "Mammoth Cheese" was sent to President Jefferson. Peale was even nicknamed "Mr. Mammoth"!

After three months of hard work, the first skeleton was finished. Peale used papier-mâché and carved wood to fill in some missing pieces,

*Charles Willson Peale himself (1741-1827), posing with a
massive leg bone from the mastodon that he discovered.*

but the finished product was impressive. What
was once a pile of muddy bones became a massive
creature fifteen feet long, eleven feet high at the
shoulder, with tusks eleven feet long! Peale first
displayed the skeleton on Christmas Eve, 1801,
following a parade down the streets of
Philadelphia.

Charles Willson Peale

Born in 1741 in Maryland, Charles Willson Peale became one of the most well-known and multitalented men of his time. He was what people often call a "Renaissance Man," meaning that he cultivated a broad range of interests, from painting to archeology. Peale was also a patriot. He served as an officer in the American Army during the American Revolution, but his achievements didn't end there.

Peale began his studies as a saddler's apprentice and learned the craft well enough to open his own shop.

It was Peale's interest in science that led him to start the new nation's first natural history museum in Philadelphia in 1786. His skill as a painter led him to paint the portraits of several of his notable contemporaries, including George Washington. Peale himself painted the scene of the mastodon dig that appears in this Postscript.

Peale's legacy continued into the next generation. Some of his 17 children became artists and scientists themselves.

Mammoths in New York State

Is New York State's Orange County the mastodon capital of the world? Some people think so. More mastodons (the scientific name for mammoth)

Peale Museum, Baltimore City Life Museums

The Exhumation of the Mastodon, *a painting that Peale made at the Masten farm dig site. The scene depicts the contraption that Peale designed to remove water from a marl pit. Powered by men walking in the wheel, the device hoisted water in the buckets that rose through its center.*

have been discovered there than in any other place in the world — over three hundred remains so far!

More than 10,000 years ago, the world was locked in an Ice Age. Glaciers covered the earth's surface. Scientists believe that the giant, shaggy creatures we now call mastodons or wooly mammoths roamed throughout North America. Large herds of mastodons lived in Orange County, near what we now call the Hudson River.

For Further Reading

Nowack, Ronald M. *Walker's Mammals of the World, Fifth Ed., Vol. 2*. Baltimore and London: Johns Hopkins, 1991.

Peale, Rembrandt. *Account of the Skeleton of the Mammoth, a Non-descript Carnivorous Animal of Immense Size found in America*. London: E. Lawrence, 1802.

Peale, Rembrandt. *An Historical Disquisition on the Mammoth, or Great American Incognitum, An Extinct, Immense, Carnivorous Animal, Whose Fossil Remains have been found in North America*. London: C. Mercier for E. Lawrence, 1803.

Be sure to look for all the other books in the Stories of the States series

NEW FOR 1994
The Children of Flight Pedro Pan
by Maria Armengol Acierno

In 1961, Maria Aleman and her brother, Jose, find themselves with a planeload of children fleeing the aftermath of the Cuban Revolution — without their parents! Bound for a new life in Miami, Maria and Jose have no idea if they'll ever see their mother and father again. And everything in America is so hard to get used to. Will they be able to make the adjustment to a totally different culture?

Drums at Saratoga
American Dreams
both by Lisa Banim

Voyage of the Half Moon
Fire in the Valley
Mr. Peale's Bones
all by Tracey West

Golden Quest
East Side Story
both by Bonnie Bader

Forbidden Friendship
by Judith Eichler Weber

DATE DUE			

J
F
Wes

West, Tracey, 1965-

Mr. Peale's bones